Make a Masterpiece

Watercolors

by Alix Wood

Gareth Stevens
PUBLISHING

Please visit our website, www.garethstevens.com. For a free color catalog of all our high-quality books, call toll free 1-800-542-2595 or fax 1-877-542-2596.

Cataloging-in-Publication Data

Names: Wood, Alix.
Title: Watercolors / Alix Wood.
Description: New York : Gareth Stevens Publishing, 2019. | Series: Make a masterpiece | Includes glossary and index.
Identifiers: ISBN 9781538235720 (pbk.) | ISBN 9781538235744 (library bound) | ISBN 9781538235737 (6pack)
Subjects: LCSH: Watercolor painting--Technique--Juvenile literature.
Classification: LCC ND2440.W66 2019 | DDC 751.42'2--dc23

First Edition

Published in 2019 by
Gareth Stevens Publishing
111 East 14th Street, Suite 349
New York, NY 10003

Produced for Gareth Stevens by Alix Wood Books
Designed by Alix Wood
Editor: Eloise Macgregor
Consultant: Richard Mabey, watercolor and ink artist

Photo credits:
Cover and title page background, 3, 5 top, 6 top © Adobe Stock Images; 4 @ Worcester Art Museum; all other images © Alix Wood

Printed in the United States of America

CPSIA compliance information: Batch #CW19GS For further information contact Gareth Stevens, New York, New York at 1-800-542-2595.

Contents

What Is Watercolor?

Watercolor is a paint that is mixed with water. It is a **transparent** paint, which means it is see-through. If you paint one color over the top of another, you won't completely cover the first color like you will with some other paints. Watercolor artists make lighter colors by adding water, instead of white paint. The wet paint colors will often mix and move around the paper, creating unexpected effects. This is all part of the fun of painting with watercolors!

This painting, "Muddy Alligators," by American artist John Singer Sargent, is painted using watercolors. If you look closely, you can see his pencil marks under the transparent paint.

What Will You Need?

▶ Watercolor Paint
You can buy watercolor paint individually in tubes, or **pans**. You can also buy sets of paint.

mixing palette lid

▶ A Place to Mix Paint
Paint sets usually have a mixing **palette** in the lid. If you don't have one of these, you'll need somewhere to mix your paint. A plastic plate works well.

▶ Watercolor Paper
Buy the best paper you can afford. Paper can have a rough or a smooth surface. Smooth paper is either hot or cold pressed. Hot-pressed paper is very smooth. Cold-pressed has a little texture, and is often called "not" paper, meaning it is "not hot-pressed." You can buy different thicknesses of paper, too. A 140 lb, or 300 **gsm** weight, cold-pressed paper is a good option.

▶ Brushes
You'll need a large brush for **washes**, and a finer brush for detail. A silicone brush can be useful, too.

a rough-textured watercolor paper

You will also need paper towels, white acrylic paint, plastic wrap, some masking tape, a wax crayon or masking fluid, and some salt.

Mixing Colors

The most useful watercolor paints to buy are a red, a blue, and a yellow. You can mix all the colors you need with just these three **primary** colors. Try painting three overlapping circles, like in the picture below, and learn all about color mixing.

1 Create a puddle of yellow paint and paint a circle on some paper. Let it dry completely.

2 Then paint a red circle, overlapping the yellow one. Where the red and yellow colors overlap creates an orange color.

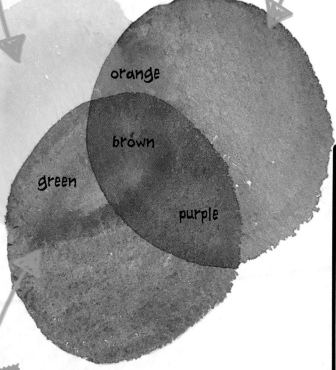

orange

brown

green

purple

3 Once your red circle is completely dry, paint a blue circle overlapping both the yellow and the red circle. Now you have created green, brown, and purple!

TIP

If you want to create a black, first mix a brown in your palette using your three colors. Don't add too much water. Then add more blue. Adjust the mix until you get a rich, dark color. You may need to add a little more of the red or yellow.

To make gray, just add a little water to your black.

So Many Blues!

To make lighter **tints** of any of your colors, you just need to add some water. Try painting this strip of different blues. Mix a small puddle of blue using just a tiny bit of water and paint a small square. Add a little water to your puddle using your brush, and paint the next square. Keep going until you have barely any color in your puddle at all. The colors will look lighter once they have dried.

To make darker shades of a color, mix in some dark gray instead of water. See page 6 to see how to mix gray. Gradually adding gray to a blue will create increasingly darker blues. Try it with some other colors, too.

Master Class

Different Ways to Mix Color

If you want a **uniform** color, it is best to mix paint in a palette. You can mix colors directly on paper, or by using a **glaze**, too. A glaze is when you paint over the top of a dry layer of paint, like our circles on page 6. As watercolor is see-through, a glaze looks a little like different-colored sheets of glass placed on top of each other. To mix color directly on your paper, drop a wet color onto another wet color. You can watch the two colors mix in front of your eyes!

green mixed on the paper

green mixed using a glaze

All About Washes

Large areas are usually painted using one of three types of wash. A flat wash is the same color all over. A graded wash changes from a dark color to a lighter color. A variegated wash changes from one color to another. Do you think you can master each of these washes?

A Flat Wash

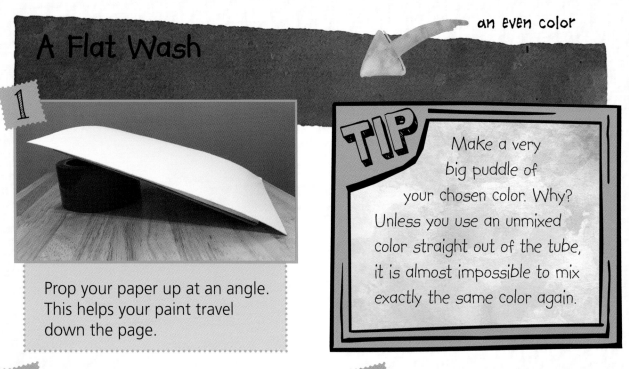

an even color

1

Prop your paper up at an angle. This helps your paint travel down the page.

TIP

Make a very big puddle of your chosen color. Why? Unless you use an unmixed color straight out of the tube, it is almost impossible to mix exactly the same color again.

2

Fill a large brush with your paint. Pull the brush across the top of the paper. At the bottom of your brushstroke you should see a line of puddled paint.

3

Add more paint to your brush. Overlap the bead of paint as you make your next brushstroke. Continue like this to the bottom of the paper.

A Graded Wash

color getting paler or stronger

1 Load your brush and paint a few strokes across the paper, just like you did for your flat wash.

2 Add a little water to your paint. Overlap the bead of paint as you make your next brushstroke. Add more water with each brushstroke.

A Variegated Wash

changing from one color to another

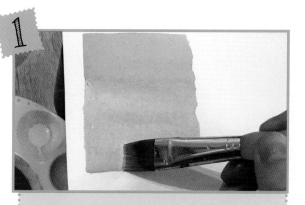

1 Mix big puddles of paint in your chosen colors. Paint a few strokes of one color. Wash your brush and fill it with your second color. Overlap the bead of paint as you paint. Change color as many times as you wish.

Paper Towel Clouds

You will need a palette or saucer to mix your colors on, a large watercolor brush, a jar of clean water, a sponge, paper towels, and some watercolor paper. Don't forget to prop your paper up at a bit of an angle before you paint.

1

Dip your brush into clean water and drip a little water into your palette. Fill your brush with blue paint and add it to your puddle. Add more water using your brush until you have a big puddle of blue paint.

2

Create your sky using a graded wash. Make a brushstroke across the top of your paper. Keep adding a little water to your paint puddle as you work down the paper. Your paper may **buckle** at this stage. If you are using good, thick watercolor paper, it should flatten out again once it is dry.

3

While your paint is still wet, scrunch up a piece of paper towel. Starting at the top of your sky, gently blot out a few little cloud shapes. Look at a cloudy sky to see the shapes and sizes you might want to paint.

4

With your paint still wet, add some darker areas to the top of the sky, and some pink or yellow sunset colors near the bottom. Let your painting dry. You can speed up this process by asking an adult to dry your painting using a hair dryer.

5

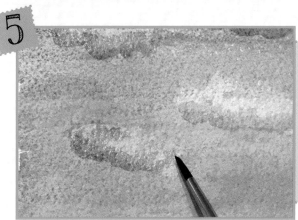

Once your painting is completely dry, mix a little light gray paint. Paint some shadows along the bottom of your clouds. Then soften the edges of your gray shadows using a small wet brush to blend the paint upward.

When we say "completely dry," the paint must be really dry. If it's still damp, your brush will lift the paint beneath as you try to add more color.

Sunset over the Sea

Watercolors are great for painting **landscapes** and **seascapes**. Using some of the techniques you have already learned, try painting this sunset over the sea. You will need good watercolor paper, paint, a thick and thin brush, and two jars of clean water.

1

With your paper at an angle, and a large brush, create a variegated wash from blue to yellow. Dab out a few clouds. Add some red and yellow sunset colors. Let it dry.

2
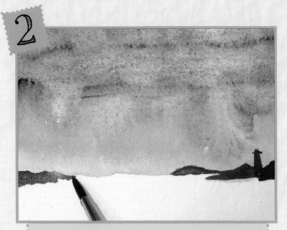

Once your sky is completely dry, mix a gray and add some rocks and a lighthouse along the **horizon**. You could add a yellow setting sun between the rocks.

3

To paint the sea, dry your brush and put just a little blue paint on it. As you drag the brush across the paper, it should leave white gaps, which look like light reflecting on your water!

TIP

The sea reflects the colors in the sky. Use the same colors for both and your sea will look realistic.

4

Paint the rest of your sea using the same blue as your sky. Add dabs of the other sunset colors under where they appear in your sky, so the sea reflects the sky.

5

Mix a dark gray color. Once your painting is completely dry, paint a boat. Then paint a squiggly line under the boat, which is its reflection in the water.

Masking

With watercolors, sometimes you may want to **mask** areas of your paper so they do not get covered in paint. There are a few different ways you can do this.

▶ Masking Tape

Masking tape is a special tape that isn't too sticky. This makes it easy to lift off your paper when you have finished using it to mask an area.

▶ Masking Fluid

This liquid dries into a rubber-like state. You can paint it on using a small brush, so it is great for masking delicate thin lines. Once dry, it protects the paper from the paint and then can easily be peeled or rubbed off.

▶ Wax Crayon Resist

Wax **resists** watercolor paint. It covers the area of paper and keeps the paint from being able to make contact with the surface. Afterward, you can either leave the crayon on the paper, or carefully scrape it away with a fingernail.

▶ Paper Cutouts

Cut out the area you want to paint from a sheet of paper. The rest of the paper will then mask the area you want to keep paint-free.

Master Class

Masking Practice

Create a picture using all these masking techniques.

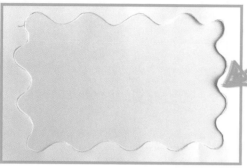

Take two sheets of paper. Cut out an interesting frame shape from one sheet. Place your frame over the second sheet. Secure it in place on the back using masking tape.

Write a name or word using masking tape. Cut or rip the tape to make the letters. It doesn't matter how messy your tape looks, as long as the shape of the letters is right.

Draw some patterns using masking fluid or wax crayon. Masking fluid dries like glue, so use an old paintbrush and wash your brush with soap right after use.

Mix up two or three colors and start to paint. Hold down your frame as you paint near it, so your brush doesn't accidentally poke underneath. Once your painting is completely dry, remove all your masking.

Spider on a Cobweb

You can use masking fluid or a white wax crayon to create a picture of a delicate spider's web. If you are using wax crayon, draw your cobweb in good light, so you can see where you have made your marks.

1

If you are using masking fluid to draw your web, use an old paintbrush, or a silicone brush like this one.

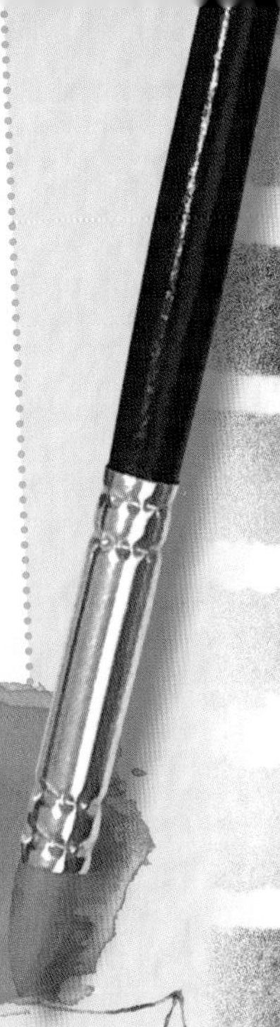

Look at some pictures of cobwebs. Draw your web using a sharp wax crayon or masking fluid.

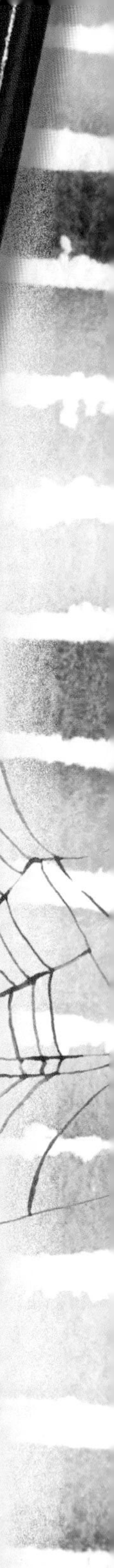

2

If you used masking fluid, wait until it is completely dry. If it is still wet it will smudge and clog up your paintbrush. Mix some background colors, and paint all over your paper.

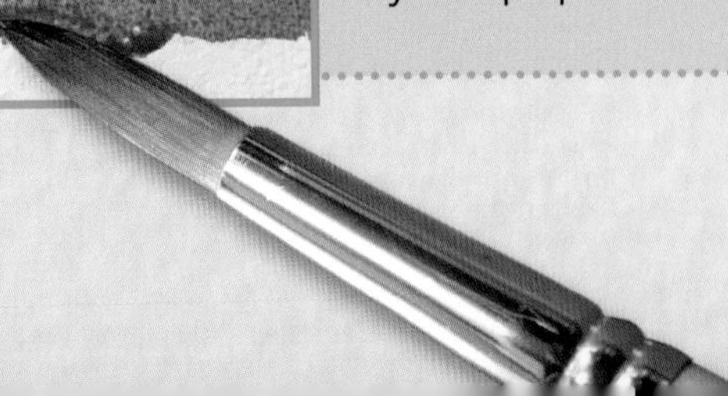

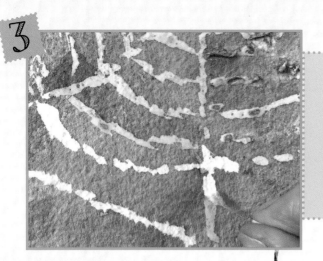

3

It is very important to wait until the paint is completely dry before peeling off the masking fluid. Otherwise you may pull off some of the paint or the paper, too.

4

Mix up some black paint. Choose a place to paint your spider. If you used wax crayon, you will need to place it away from your crayon web, as the crayon will resist the paint.

TIP

If you used wax crayon and can't find any space to paint your spider, use acrylic paint instead. Unlike watercolor, it will paint over the wax.

Fun with Texture

There are some great tricks you can use with watercolor to make different textures. Try some of these in your next painting.

Using Salt

1

Paint a wash on your paper. Let the paint dry a little. Sprinkle some salt onto the paint. Let the paint dry completely.

2

Once the paint is dry, brush the salt off the paper. The salt soaks up the paint, leaving a white, spotted texture.

Brush Spatters

1

Cover a large area with newspaper and wear old clothes. Mix a few paint colors.

2

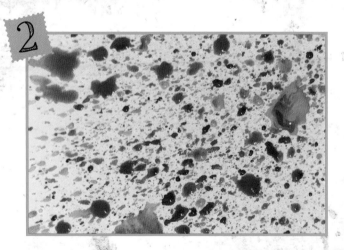

Dip an old toothbrush in paint and run your thumb along the bristles. The paint will spatter onto your paper.

Rubbing Alcohol

Keep the windows open when you use rubbing alcohol, or it can make you feel ill.

1 Mix two or three strong paint colors. Loosely paint your paper with the wet paint.

2 Dip a cotton swab into the rubbing alcohol. Dot the alcohol onto your paper.

Plastic Wrap

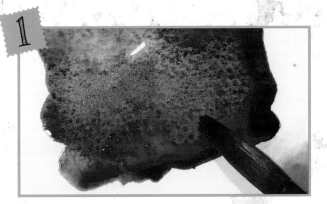

1 Cover your paper in splotches of different-colored paint.

2 Press scrunched plastic wrap onto your paper. When the paint is completely dry, lift off the wrap.

TIP It can be helpful to make a sample page showing all the techniques you have tried. Write how you made each effect, so you can refer to it when you do a painting.

19

Winter Snowman

Use your salt and paint spatter techniques to create this snowy picture. Brushing the sky with water first helps the colors blend and mix in those areas. To create the white snow foreground, leave that area of the paper dry and unpainted.

1

Draw a snowman and a horizon lightly in pencil. Brush clean water over the sky area, avoiding the ground and snowman.

2

If paint dribbles into a snow area, dab it off with a cloth.

Drop some light and dark blue paint on the sky area. Tip the paper around so the color mixes and spreads around.

3

Using a smaller brush, move the wet paint all around the outline of your snowman.

4

Using the same color as your sky, add a few shadows onto your snowman and onto the snow area.

5

To create falling snowflakes, sprinkle some salt onto the sky. Once the background is dry, rub away the salt.

6 To add more snow, you could flick on some white acrylic paint using a toothbrush. Then paint your snowman's hat, face, buttons, and arms.

Adding Ink Lines

Watercolor paintings are usually loose and flowing. You can tighten your picture up by using some ink outlines. You can add ink at the start of a painting, in the middle, or at the end. You don't need a special pen—you can use a ballpoint pen to draw with, or even a stick!

TIP Practice with your pen or stick before you start. With an ink pen, the harder you press, the thicker the line you get. Dip your pen lightly into the ink. Try drawing some thick-to-thin lines. Practice different types of lines or dots that you can use for shading areas in your drawing.

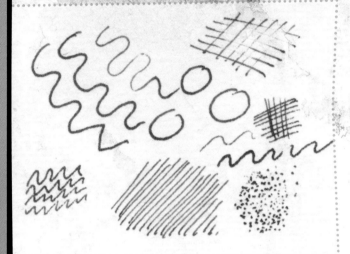

If you add ink lines and shading before you paint, you must use waterproof ink or else it will smudge.

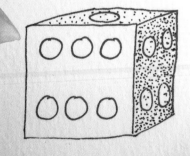

You can use any type of ink if you add ink detail after your paint, as long as the paint is dry.

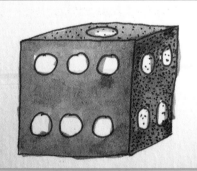

Master Class

Using Ink Before, During, and After

You will need a waterproof ink pen, like this technical drawing pen, some paper, a small brush, and watercolor paints.

Draw a house in pencil. Then go over your lines using a waterproof ink pen. Erase your pencil.

Carefully paint your house using watercolor paint.

Once the paint has completely dried, add some more detail to your windows. Paint some bush shapes. Let them dry.

Finally, maybe add some leaves, a doormat, and some brick details to your picture.

Flower Garden

An ink outline can really make your watercolor painting pop. Ink gives your painting a very different look. Try this outline idea. You can use smudgy ink if you are a careful painter, and won't accidentally paint over the ink lines. If you don't want white outlines, make sure you use waterproof ink so you can paint right up to your pen lines.

1

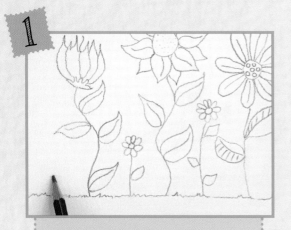

Sketch out your design using a pencil. Keep the shapes simple so they are easy to paint around.

2

Start to trace over your pencil lines with ink. We used a nib pen, but you can use a stick, a marker, or a ballpoint pen.

TIP

Water resistant ink will still smudge, but waterproof ink won't. Test your ink first by painting water over a bit. As this project has a white gap around the drawing, even water resistant ink shouldn't smudge, unless you accidentally go over the lines.

To make a more interesting ink line, try drawing a wobbly or broken line. It can add life to a natural subject like flowers or trees.

3

Once you have finished tracing the drawing, erase the pencil lines. Now you are ready to add some watercolor.

4

Mix up a big puddle of your background color. Using a smallish brush, very carefully paint around your ink lines, leaving a little white gap all around the edges.

5

If you used waterproof ink, you can go right to the edges when you paint the detail. If your ink isn't waterproof, leave a small gap. Alternatively, draw over your ink line using white crayon, which will resist the paint.

Making a Collage

Paper painted using watercolors is great to use to make a **collage**. A collage is made using different paper or fabric all arranged and stuck onto a backing to make a picture. Try using some of the techniques you have learned to create some useful collage paper.

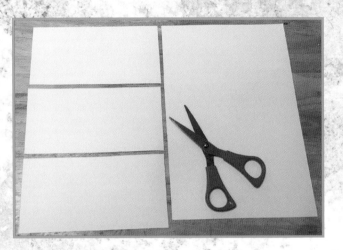

Cut a large sheet of watercolor paper in half. Then cut one of the halves into thirds. If you have more of the same paper, you may want to add another strip, so you can make more mountains (see page 27).

Cloudy Sky Background

Paint a graded wash sky at the top half of the half sheet of paper. Pick out some clouds using a paper towel. This will be your background.

Plastic Wrap Mountains

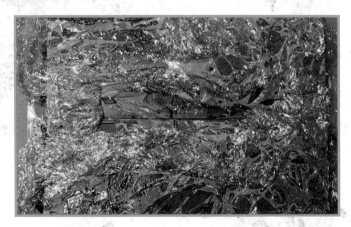

Paint splotches of purples and reds on a strip or two of your paper. Scrunch up some plastic wrap and press it onto the paint. Leave until completely dry.

Rubbing Alcohol Lake

Paint some blues and greens onto one paper strip. While the paint is damp, dab here and there with a cotton swab soaked in rubbing alcohol.

Paint Spatter Beach

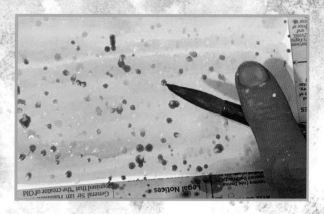

Paint a strip of paper in sandy colors. Spatter some dark browns and white onto your sand.

Master Class

Ripped Paper Collage

Use the pieces of art you made to create a lake and mountain collage. You have to be brave and rip up your great paper, but the result makes it worth it!

A Beautiful Galaxy

Use some skills you have learned to create this space collage.
Create a starry background and add a painted planet Earth.
You will need to use white acrylic paint to create the stars.
Using more than one type of paint is called "mixed **media**".

1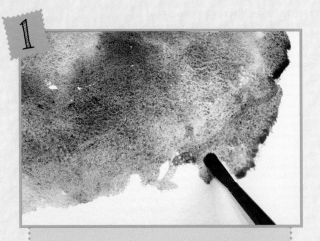

Mix up separate puddles of different blues, a purple, and a pinky red. Cover your paper in different colored splotches of paint. Use plenty of water so they run into each other.

2

Once the paint is completely dry, put on some more layers. This way you can gradually build up strong color in some areas. Leave some areas paler to look like the Milky Way.

TIP

Watercolor paint looks lighter when it dries than when it is wet. Gradually building up the layers will give you a rich, interesting background with strong colors.

3

Once you are happy with your background, spatter white acrylic paint onto your picture by gently tapping a full paintbrush.

To make your planet Earth, draw a circle on another piece of paper. It must be small enough to fit on your collage. Wet the paper with a clean brush.

Paint areas of green land and blue sea onto your Earth. Then cut out your planet and glue it in place onto your galaxy background.

Glossary

buckle To develop kinks and bend out of shape.

collage A work of art made by gluing pieces of different materials to a flat surface.

glaze A thin layer of paint laid over another layer of paint.

gsm Grams per square meter; a way of measuring the weight of paper.

horizon The line where the Earth or sea seems to meet the sky.

landscapes Pictures of natural scenery.

mask To cover an area to protect it from the paint.

media The materials that are used to create a work of art.

palette A board or dish used by a painter to lay and mix paint colors on.

pans Usually round (or rectangular), small, hard cakes of paint.

primary A group of colors, usually red, blue, and yellow, from which all other colors can be obtained by mixing.

resists Withstands the effect of an action.

seascapes Paintings of the sea.

tints Shades or varieties of a color.

transparent Fine or sheer enough to be seen through.

uniform Not varying.

washes Thin coats of paint.

Further Information

Books

Hurd, Thatcher. *Paint This Book! Watercolor for the Artistically Undiscovered.* New York, NY: The Experiment LLC, 2017.

Martin, Lisa. *The Big Book of Art: Draw! Paint! Create!: An adventurous journey into the wild & wonderful world of art!* Lake Forest, CA: Walter Foster Jr, 2015.

Websites

Art for Kids Hub video showing how to paint a fall leaf using watercolor:
www.youtube.com/watch?v=ye23IkKlc-4

Happy Family Art watercolor galaxy projects:
www.happyfamilyart.com/art-lessons/watercolor-art-lessons/
fun-watercolor-galaxy-and-space-paintings/

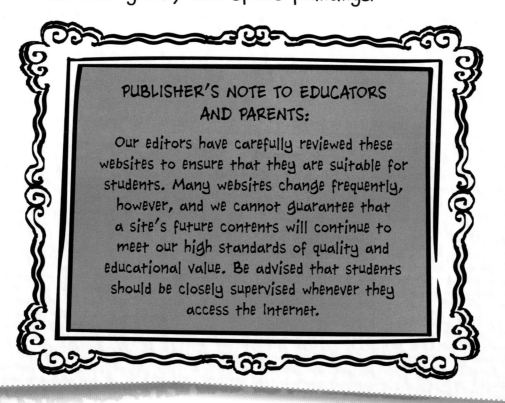

PUBLISHER'S NOTE TO EDUCATORS AND PARENTS:

Our editors have carefully reviewed these websites to ensure that they are suitable for students. Many websites change frequently, however, and we cannot guarantee that a site's future contents will continue to meet our high standards of quality and educational value. Be advised that students should be closely supervised whenever they access the Internet.

Index